The Dogs on the Beach
& Other Stories

Michael Holloway

Let's All Be There published online by Ellipsis Zine 2018.
The Devil and My Dad published in Open Pen magazine 2019.
Green Eyes was longlisted for the Sunderland Short Story Award 2019
and longlisted for the Cambridge Short Story Prize 2021.
Remember the Lake was Runner Up in the University of Liverpool
Writing Competition 2022.

Set in 11/16 pt Garamond.

Front and back cover image by Freddie Marriage from Unsplash.com,
with granted irrevocable, worldwide copyright license to use and
distribute.

www.mjdholloway.com

Front and back cover designed by Michael Holloway.

ISBN: 978-1-4709-8025-2

Printed in the United Kingdom
First Printing 2022

A Note on the Author

Michael Holloway was born in Liverpool in 1985. He studied English Literature and Creative Writing at the University of Central Lancashire and received his Masters in Creative Writing from Liverpool John Moores University. His work has appeared in various magazines, and he was shortlisted for the Sunderland Short Story Award 2018 and longlisted in 2019. He was also longlisted for the Cambridge Short Story Prize 2021. He has written a novel, which is yet to be published.

Contents

The Dogs on the Beach

It started with an Anadin. Two of them. Soon it faded and went away. Jane sat staring, drained, L-shaped like a mantis. I asked her why she always thought she was in pain but she just sat, tired-looking, tapping her fingers, so I asked her again. I said, 'Who do you think you are in so much pain?' Her eyes were pale. Her skin was pale too and I guessed she was sick but I didn't believe she was sick because she always lied. The hem of her skirt, a thin fabric, hooked at something revealing the black tights of her thighs, so I looked away.

I apologised and looked into her eyes and held my expression until she believed I was telling the truth. It had stopped raining. The window held itself in monotone as though the world outside had become anaemic. I asked her to come to the beach with me and we could make fun of the people walking their dogs. She said, 'Okay'.

It was cold outside and the air tasted of metal. She wasn't saying much, I didn't think she was enjoying the cold morning air. I said, 'Why don't you stop being so miserable, it's annoying me.'

'You don't know what it's like,' she said.

'What what's like?'

'Being me.'

'Well,' I said, 'you don't know what it's like being me. Did you ever think about that?'

'I have thought about that,' she said. 'I often wonder what it's like being you. I've imagined living your life and I've wondered what it would be like to be a man. I suppose it is difficult. You have a lot to deal with. So much testosterone. It must feel pointless. I'm glad I'm not you.'

'And I'm glad I'm not you,' I said.

She took another Anadin as we walked. I thought she shouldn't have taken any more.

'I don't like coming up here,' Jane said. 'My dad used to take me up here when I was little. I never liked it because it was always too cold and I didn't like the water.'

'Don't worry, we won't go onto the beach.'

'But these places seem like places you can get lost. I know it sounds stupid but, I don't know, it's easy for things to go wrong.'

'There won't be many people down there. You're completely safe.'

'How do you suppose some people get away with it?'

'With what?'

'Suppose you were walking around in the dark at home and someone comes up behind you and you panic and kill them. The lights come on and it's your own father.'

'Why would that even happen?'

'I'm just supposing,' she said. 'Suppose that happened. Suppose you killed your own father. You'd become the man of the house. An ironic punishment for lashing out in the dark, killing your own dad. Ironic, isn't it?'

We got to the beach. The morning hung heavy. There was a strange dull greyness, a peculiar inwardness suppressed by our silence and Jane's mood suppressed with Anadin and bottled water. I was curious what was the cause of her pain. 'You,' she said.

'Me?' I said.

'You're causing my pain,' she said. She didn't say anything after that, although I questioned her over and over to be replied with silence. Her eyes followed the swans and the crows. The wind pushed apart her hair and she smiled. I asked what it was she smiling at but she didn't say anything. I thought maybe she was mad at me for some reason and I tried to think back to what I had done or said but I couldn't think of anything. It was even colder on the beach. The sky seemed asleep, the colour purple pushed like a birth through the clouds after the rain so the sand was a dark gold and the people were few and the dogs were just lively creatures jumping about with black or red collars and the white non-shining sun like a moon cast dingy morose shadows like people's moods long over the sand which doubled them and doubled the dogs so that the dogs now ran in pairs.

She took an Anadin. I said, 'You shouldn't take any more of those.'

'You're not my dad,' she said.

'I know I'm not,' I said.

I watched her take the pill, swallow the water, gulp. I watched her breathe and shiver. I watched her breathe out and in, the curious way her shoulders slouched forward while she thought no one was looking, the way she didn't smile when she didn't feel the need. To her, I was a liar as much as she was. She looked at me and smiled and I was glad.

Two people walked on the beach. 'Look at them,' she said. 'You think they're married?'

'No,' I said. 'Divorced. He's trailing behind her, see? He's desperate for her to sign the divorce papers.' She laughed.

'How desperate can you be to want someone to leave you?'

'I think some people are like that.'

'If someone wanted to leave me I'd let them.'

After a while it began to rain and I suggested we head back but Jane didn't want to go. We decided to go onto the beach, walking along the hard, wet sand. She walked ahead of me and

3

said something about the dogs.

'What did you say?' I said. 'About the dogs.'

'I said, why do people feel the need to bring their dogs to the beach?'

'I don't know,' I said. 'I don't think the dogs belong to them.'

'You don't?'

'I don't think the dogs belong to anyone.'

'You mean like stray dogs?'

'No, I mean like, look at them.' I pointed at the dogs on the beach. They were wandering like free things. They were happy and obedient with a sense of curiosity and fear. And the people with them. They too were generally happy. They were obedient and they too had a sense of curiosity and fear. They all poked around the sand like dogs. Every single one of them.

We walked further in the rain and over by the cliff wall there was a body in the sand. We both stood there staring. It was a dead girl. Her skin was pale blue and her eyes were closed and she looked quite young. It seemed she was sleeping. It seemed like her face was just a mask half-buried in the sand. Jane held my hand. 'What should we do?' she said.

'Just leave it,' I said.

'Shouldn't we tell someone?'

'No.'

'But someone's probably missing her. We should tell someone.'

There was an old couple on the beach. They were walking a dog which ran ahead of them. I didn't like them; they were everything we weren't. The dog saw us and ran over to us. It seemed incredibly happy to see us as if it was an old friend. Jane stroked it in a childish way and she looked happy. 'I wish I had a

4

dog,' she said. She held it tightly around the neck until it whimpered but it still wagged its tail. The dog turned and sniffed at the dead girl and nosed at the clump of seaweed tangled in her hair. I wondered who the girl was, but to us it didn't matter. We just hovered on the verge of moving and not moving.

'I'm going to pull her out of the sand,' Jane said. But she didn't. I waited for her to do it but she didn't. She just took another Anadin and stared at the girl as small grains of sand blew across her dead face. I thought maybe Jane was jealous of the dead girl but I didn't know why. I guess she thought she was like her. As if we were all unidentified bodies. Or nameless and ignorant like dogs on the beach. The old couple stood in the distance watching us. The dog ran back to them.

The Devil and My Dad

Mrs Feldman's husband died and she was having a hard time coping with it. She was an old lady with grey hair. She was thin and had no colour in her eyes as if she had no soul, which made me and my brother think she wasn't really human. Mrs Feldman was also our schoolteacher. She'd taught geography for 35 years. That was a long time. She was a nice lady because she didn't act like a teacher outside of class since we just saw her as one of our neighbours.

She told us things about her dead husband, Joe, who was in the war, she said, and fought the Germans and she used to tell us about the hard time Joe had, because he was a Jew, and that was to do with the war, because people were killing Jews and Joe Feldman was fighting the Nazis who wanted to kill him. That's why I always looked up to Mr Feldman when he was alive, though he wasn't as nice as Mrs Feldman. He was a miserable old man and mean and never talked to me or my brother, Samuel. He always kept our ball when we kicked it over the fence, and one time he caught my brother climbing over and my brother fell onto the other side. Mr Feldman came out and my brother screamed and I screamed for my brother but we were separated by the fence and I imagined I was like one of those Jews in the concentrating camps that Mrs Feldman told us about, and Mr Feldman took my brother away into his house, and I ran through our house, outside, round the front and to the Feldman's front door. I banged on the door screaming that the Nazis were going to kill my brother and Mr Feldman opened the door and I screamed and my brother ran out screaming and Mr Feldman didn't move from the doorstep. I guess he was fed up with the screaming. He must have told our parents because they grounded us both the next day. I had to apologise for screaming the word Nazi outside the Feldman's house.

During this time, me and my brother had to visit Mrs Feldman to keep her company since Mum said she was impressed that Mr Feldman was dead. I didn't know why. I thought she seemed sad all the time since he died, though I suppose it would be impressive to die of lung cancer instead of being gassed by the Nazis.

It was boring when we visited Mrs Feldman. We didn't know what to do or say to her so me and Samuel made a deal to take it in turns so only one of us visited her and the other one could play in the street. And it worked out well. For the next few months, either me or my brother visited Mrs Feldman while the other one played outside with the other kids. I hated it when I had to visit her because I could see Samuel through the window on his bike and I laughed at him when he fell. Mrs Feldman heard me laughing and she said, 'Boy, what are you laughing at?'

'My brother fell off his bike.'

'Oh, well you shouldn't laugh when someone falls an' hurts themself. 'Specially if it's your brother. Even though it might look funny.' She smiled. She hadn't really smiled since Mr Feldman died. Actually, she hadn't smiled at all.

Mrs Feldman was funny. She spoke to me like she was a little kid too. It was like she hadn't really grown up, or that she just remembered what it was like being a kid. She told me these stupid jokes and we just laughed about anything even when it wasn't funny. I think it was that *she'd* said it or the timing, yeah, she had good comedy timing. I wondered if she'd ever been a comedian, but I never asked her.

Me and my brother had these bets and whoever lost had

7

to go see Mrs Feldman. But I didn't mind when I lost. I started to like going to see Mrs Feldman, so I started losing the bets on purpose.

We played Scrabble or something and she'd tell me what it was like growing up on the street when she was a kid since she'd lived on the same street her whole life, and the place sounded weird, like she was making it up, like the 1940s was just fiction in a book or something. But it didn't matter if she was making it up or not. I liked spending time with her. She was my friend.

Mrs Feldman died. I remember when it happened. She was singing. I don't know what song it was – she always liked those old-fashioned songs that sounded like they were stuck on the radio forever – but then she made weird coughing noises and fell down. I was on my own when she died. My brother was playing outside. I just stood there, looking at her, wondering what she was doing. I know that sounds stupid, but I just had this thought in my head that said, 'What's she doing?'

A week later was my tenth birthday and I felt sad because it was my birthday and Mrs Feldman wasn't there. I didn't even know what being dead was. Now I do. It means going away. That's all it means.

A few weeks after my birthday, Mr Black moved into the Feldman's old house. Mr Black was the Devil. That's what I thought of him. It's what I would have thought of anyone moving into the Feldman's old house. It wasn't right. I couldn't bear to see him move his stuff into their house. Mr Black was tall and sad-looking with pillow-creases on his cheeks as if he slept a lot. He walked over Mrs Feldman's daffodils; their necks broke under his feet. Their sad daffodil faces looking at me as if they were Mrs Feldman crying and I burst out crying and I hated Mr Black because I imagined he was the one who killed Mr and Mrs

8

Feldman. Later I had to apologise to Mr Black for calling him a Nazi.

One day I said to my brother, 'Mr Black has no family.'

'How do you know?' he said.

'Well he's not with anyone. Looks like he's going to be living on his own. He mustn't have any family.'

'Maybe he has a wife somewhere else.'

'So he's remorsed?'

'For who?' Samuel said.

'His wife.'

'You mean *div*orced.'

'Yeah.'

'I don't know.'

'He has no one.'

'He must have a mum and dad somewhere.'

'He just looks lonely,' I said. 'He looks like those sorts of people who don't have anyone and don't want anyone.'

Samuel was one year older than me. He told me I was always thinking out loud. Mrs Feldman used to tell me I should write a book. Mr Feldman used to tell me to be quiet.

A month later my dad made friends with Mr Black when Mr Black's car wouldn't start. My dad helped start it because my dad was a mechanic and could build or fix anything and Mr Black thanked him and invited my dad to drink beer in his house. So he did. I told Mum but she was happy my dad had made a new friend and she wouldn't listen to what I had to say about Mr Black, so me and Samuel went to Mr Black's front lawn and looked through the window and saw my dad and Mr Black drinking beer in the kitchen and they were laughing and they soon became good friends and they were always drinking beer in Mr Black's house and they were always laughing.

It was a Sunday. I was playing in the street with Samuel and our dog, Bentley. Bentley was running up and down the street with a ball and Mum called us in for dinner and we left him outside and when we went back outside we found Bentley's dead body on the road.

'Oh, a car must have hit him,' Mum said. But no cars ever came up our road, not that day anyway. It was completely deserted. Mr Black looked at us through his window. He just stood there staring at us, stood in the place Mr Feldman used to stand. It was weird that he was in their house. He was trespassing. He didn't belong there.

Later that day my dad went next door to Mr Black's to drink beer and laugh and me and Samuel buried Bentley in the front lawn and Dad and Mr Black came outside to drink beer in the sun. Mr Black came over and leaned on the fence. He was thin and he wore a suit. 'What are you boys up to, then?' he said. This was probably the first time he'd actually spoken to us. I was used to him just staring at us through the window. His voice was cold and dry. He sounded like he had a sore throat, like he was sick or something.

'Burying Bentley,' I said.

'Who's Bentley?'

'Our dog.'

'Oh. How did Bentley die?'

'I don't know. We just found him dead.'

'These things happen. Dogs often die. You can't help it.' Mr Black turned around and walked over to Dad and they sat on deck chairs and drank beer in the sun. Samuel made a grave with sticks and I tried to scratch Bentley's name on it, but it didn't look very good.

Mum began to get annoyed with my dad because he

started going to the pub with Mr Black and they wouldn't come back for hours. Sometimes they wouldn't come back until the next day and my parents would start arguing and Mr Black would just go inside his own house without saying a word and wait until my dad would knock on his door again.

One day, Samuel asked me if I thought about Mr and Mrs Feldman.

'Why ask me that?' I said.

'You don't even talk about them anymore,' he said. 'It's as if they were never even here.'

'I just don't want to talk about them.'

'You've forgotten them.'

'I haven't.'

'Talk about them.'

'What do you want me to say?'

'Tell me where they've gone.'

Sometimes I wondered why I was the younger brother when Samuel talked to me like this, expecting me to give him all the answers.

Mr Black stood over us and answered Samuel, 'They've gone to Hell.' We looked up and saw the skull-shape of his head, the road-mark lines of his wrinkles, sharp cheekbones and chin the colour of ash, colourless eyes so similar to Mrs Feldman's it frightened me. 'Or Heaven,' he said, shrugging his shoulders.

'I don't know if Hell or Heaven are real places,' Samuel said.

'They are,' Mr Black said. 'You can go to those places while you're still alive. You can be on your way to anywhere and then all of a sudden you're standing in the middle of Hell and you can't get out.'

'We're not supposed to talk to you,' I said.

11

'Are you the Devil?' Samuel said.

'Yes,' Mr Black said and walked away. He walked to his house and shut the door. Soon after that, Dad came outside looking tired and we said 'Hi' to him but he didn't reply. He knocked on Mr Black's front door and Mr Black let him in. He went inside and Mr Black looked at us as he closed the door. All they seemed to do was drink beer. Later they came out and got in Dad's car and drove away. It was getting late and the sky was orange. It cast a light over Bentley's grave so the cross marked an X on the grass. The X slowly moved across the yard as the sun set and sat on Mr Black's house and stayed there for some time.

My dad died. He was in a car accident with Mr Black. Mr Black said sorry to my mum and to me and Samuel and he disappeared into his house for a long time. I told Samuel that Dad died because he was driving with the Devil.

When winter came and it got cold, Mr Black went for walks. Mum was still grieving. I think I was finished grieving. Samuel had a bit of grieving left to do but only because he was sad a lot more often. I followed Mr Black one day and he walked to the park and sat on a bench. He saw me and waved and looked down at his feet as I walked over to him. I thought his wave would be evil as if he was a villain from the films me and Samuel saw in the cinema, but it wasn't. He was just a man. He said, 'You're a good boy, and so's your brother, but you won't be that way forever.'

'What do you mean?'

'I mean that you'll grow up and change.'

'Will Samuel still like me?'

'I don't know.'

'I thought you were the Devil.'

'If I were the Devil, would I be talking to you right now?

You have a vivid imagination. You should write a book.'

'Mrs Feldman once told me to write a book.'

'Who's Mrs Feldman?'

'She used to live in your house.'

'Oh. I never met her,' he said. 'I'm sorry about your dad.'

Mr Black got up and left. I sat on the bench and it was cold. I listened to the trees moving around. I could still smell Mr Black's medicinal beer smell. I could hear his voice and I could hear my dad's voice. Later, I saw a dead sparrow. It had fallen from the sky. It lay on the ground, its feet curled up, its eyes closed. I looked at the sparrow for a long time and thought about my dad and I thought about where I could possibly end up when I die. I buried the sparrow in the grass, amongst the moving trees in the wind.

Canal Turn

In the evening, the police questioned me about the horse and
the boy. It was an accident. A boy drowning underneath a
racehorse was unheard of. Almost funny if it weren't for his
sobbing mother leaning on a policeman's shoulder.

'Emily,' I said. 'Make sure you get home to your
mother.'

'I will,' the girl said, and walked off. It was dark now
and the sky was purple like a fresh bruise. It was just about
spring and the evening was pretty. Birds still awake, twittering in
the branches.

I waited there for a long time as hundreds of smartly
dressed drunk people walked past on the far side of the road.
They'd been at the races all day and were heading into town to
enjoy the night. Some looked over. Barefoot women stopped in
the street when they saw him, or the shape of him, under the
sheet.

Earlier that day, it was cold and bright. There were bulbs
sprouting on the tree branches. It was April and the cheering
and screaming fell from up the hill. I'd been in work all day and
I was tired. I sold bathroom fittings for a living. Pipes, u-bends,
sinks, toilets, things like that. My ex-wife used to work in the
shop with me before she moved away. We'd met in the shop and
we worked together for a year before I took her out on a date. It
was another five years before we married. We had a daughter,
and we were living our lives as if we'd always known each other.
It had been some time since I'd seen either of them.

It was the girl who'd called to me. I ignored her at first; when I'm in that mood, no one matters to me except myself and I just wanted to get home and sit down in front of the TV. But she kept on shouting 'Hey,' so I thought I'd go down and have a look.

I turned off from the street and walked towards the canal. They were only young. Still in the grey colours of their school uniform. The girl didn't look older than fifteen. The boy's white untucked shirt was filthy and wet.

The girl's hair was tied in a ponytail. The sun shone on her so that her hair became a lighter shade of brown. Her eyes were red with bloodshot. The boy looked straight through me. It didn't seem like his brow could fold any thicker than it was.

'What is it?' I said. 'What do you want?' I looked at her then the boy. I waited for a moment for either of them to respond. The girl was preoccupied with something, but they just stared at me. I was a little unnerved by the boy. He was tall, maybe six-foot-something and could have probably overpowered me given the chance. I wasn't young anymore and I wouldn't have been very agile in my suit anyway.

'The horse,' the girl said.

The words didn't register. The word itself – *horse* – didn't make sense as though it had deconstructed into the basic Latin symbols for the animal.

'It's the horse,' the girl said. 'Check if it's dead.'

'What horse?' I said.

The cold sun struck her thin arm pointing towards the canal. I looked to where she pointed. In the canal, on the far side, the large head of a horse poked out of the water. It glistened like ice and wasn't struggling at all. It was snagged on some branches and roots. Its heavy body was under the water.

The black eyes stared at something but I realised they weren't seeing anything.

'Jesus Christ,' I said. 'How'd that get in there?'

'Help it,' the girl said.

'He can't help it,' the boy said.

'It looks like it's dead,' I said.

'Would you tell *her* that?' the boy said. I was surprised to finally hear his voice. He sounded older than he looked. In a way, I was glad he'd spoken. The soft sloshing of water, the exact sound of how I would wash myself in the sink at home, washed over the horse's unblinking face.

I turned to face the girl and said, 'It's dead. I'm sorry.'

'But it was okay before,' she said. She started crying, the noise she made like an ensnared rabbit, and as the boy comforted her, he looked at me as though I'd upset her. 'It was okay before,' she said. 'It was splashing around in the water, trying to get out.'

'I'm sorry,' I said.

The boy held the girl's shoulders, his thin fingers gripped like the branches that had caught on the horse's neck. He looked deep into her eyes as though he was going to say something, but he didn't say anything. In the distance, the screaming and shouting had died down. He gently pushed her aside and she turned away and sat down with her back against the wall. She didn't seem to care how dirty it was, the damp moss blanketed the bricks behind her.

'Hey,' the boy said. 'You're going to help me.'

'With what?' I said, but I guessed what he meant.

'I'll get a stick,' he said. 'Wait there.'

He turned and walked up the path. He had a long stride so that he made quite a lot of distance in a short space of time. I looked at the girl and then at the horse. The noise up the hill was gone and there was a moment of cold silence in the air. Bare branches rustled and shook their buds. Two birds sat on a branch looking at the horse in the canal then flew away. I looked at the girl again. She sniffed. Her knees were up to her chin and she held onto her legs so that she was shaped into a ball that could easily roll away.

I struggled to think of something to say to her. I said, 'You look a lot like my daughter.'

She looked up at me.

'You're about the same age.'

'What's her name?' she asked.

'My daughter? Mary.'

'Mine's Emily.'

'Nice to meet you, Emily. I'm John.'

'I don't know anyone called Mary.'

'I didn't think you'd know her,' I said. 'You probably go to a different school.'

It was cooler down by the canal than it was up on the road. I began to feel it under my shirt. The boy had been gone longer than I thought he'd be, but I didn't want to leave the girl. Sunlight lit the wet skin of her cheeks.

'You saw it die?' I said.

'How does a horse get in a canal anyway?' she said.

'It must be a racehorse,' I said. 'You know, you do look a lot like my daughter.'

'What's she like? Is she like me?'

'I don't see her anymore.'

'How come?'

'She and her mother moved away a few years ago,' I said.

'What happened?'

'You know, the only way to get that horse out is to drain the canal,' I said. 'They use stop planks to dam the water. Empty it out to get rid of all the debris that's left. Then it all comes flooding back.'

'How can we do that?'

'It's not a job we can do,' I said. 'It takes a lot of work, lowering in the planks and draining the water.'

'Can you call someone?'

I looked up the canal. There was just the narrow stretch of water and the walls on either side lined with green moss. When I turned back, the boy was heading towards us. He was carrying two large tree branches. His smile was annoying, like he'd solved everything and wanted to be congratulated. He had a way of walking, swaying his shoulders with each step, chin elevated to make him seem taller, his chest puffed out.

'Look what I found,' he said. The girl ignored him. 'We can pull it from the roots.'

'And then what?' I said. 'Drag it out of the water? Do you have any idea how much a horse weighs?'

'Here,' he said, handing me one of the sticks.

'He says he can drain the canal,' the girl said to the boy.

'I can't do that,' I said. 'But that's what will have to be done.'

The boy looked at me with an indifference that was hard to read. A shadow deepened around his nose and mouth, and the dark of thin greasy pubescent stubble above his lip quivered as he smiled. 'Go on then,' he said. 'Drain it.'

'I can't, I don't know how.'

The boy huffed.

I watched him reach the branch with both hands over to the horse, awkwardly poking at the branches but not doing much good. Emily watched from where she sat. I decided to give it a go too, so I reached the stick over the canal; I seemed to have a better grip of it than he did. My stick prodded the horse. It disgusted me when I felt little resistance from its thick muscular neck. It gave me the sensation that I was hurting it, that it might cry out in pain if I carried on, but it didn't. I tried to release it from the branches and we both tried hacking them and untying them methodically with our sticks. I broke out in a sweat. I could then smell it. The musk. Not me, the horse. Like a dog. The yeasty smell emanating from its skin. Black eyes pleading with me to free it. I finally hooked my stick on one of the larger roots which had hooked onto the saddle under the water, and as I pulled, the horse immediately sank.

Emily shouted something and came over to the canal's edge and all three of us watched the water. It seemed deep and black now. Like oil. I doubted we'd see the horse again, almost as though it had never been there. Soon, among Emily's sobs, the horse appeared a little downstream. It bobbed a little closer to our side and stayed there.

The boy ran up the short distance to where the horse was. I watched him crouch down and reach for it. He moaned as he strained, trying to reach and the more he reached, the more distorted he became. He looked like Adam reaching out to God's hand. The boy was so close now that his fingernails just about grazed the horse's wet mane.

I didn't speak to his mother afterwards. She didn't know who I was or that I'd seen her son die. By the time Emily was gone and the crowd from the races had dispersed, I headed home. The police said they might call me in for questioning the next day.

That night, I lay in bed thinking about my daughter and her mother. It was dark enough to feel blind like my eyes could only grasp small slivers of light through dirty water. I felt restless. The stink of salt and mud still lingered on my hands. I called her. Her voice sounded tired when she spoke.

'Christ, John, it's after midnight,' she said. 'Mary's asleep.'

'I just wanted to talk.'

'You're drunk.'

'I'm not drunk,' I said. 'I just felt like calling. I made a mistake.'

'Obviously.'

'How are you?' I said. 'How's Mary?'

She sighed heavily down the phone so that it crackled. 'She doesn't want to talk to you,' she said.

'I didn't even try,' I said.

'You never did,' she said.

'I just wanted things to be better for her.'

She Was a Fan of Edward G. Robinson

I ordered Jennifer a white wine and one for myself. I hated wine. Hated the way it tasted. We drank them for a few moments under the heavy lights of the restaurant. She sat opposite me wearing a black dress, her black hair, curly and long, hanging down to her shoulders, just grazing the skin there each time she moved to drink her wine.

We were immersed in this sea of awkward attractiveness. Ever since I laid eyes on her when I began working at the furniture store three years ago, I'd wanted this. I still felt the impulsion to end up here, as though this was an inevitable part of our relationship.

Jennifer was about the same height as me and always wore black as though every workday was a funeral. I wasn't surprised to see her in black this evening. Her eyes were also dark, the sharp whites like two moons: one like light reflected on the still water of a pond, the other in the deep black of the sky. I was often taken aback by her eyes because she had the habit of staring, sometimes not realising she was doing it.

She stared at me from across the table. She smiled when I ordered white wine for us both because it's not something I usually drink. The drinks arrived quickly. We then ordered food and I ordered for her. 'Why are you ordering for me?' she said.

'I don't know,' I said. 'I was just being polite.'

'Well, I can order for myself,' she said in a thick Cambridgeshire drawl. She snorted as she laughed and called the waiter back and ordered the Penne al Salmone for herself.

She brushed back her curls and they hung lightly behind one ear. A round gold earring twinkled in the warm, ambient glow. Hot baking bread and sweet butter melting on top of it. The persistent smell of salt, maybe from the salami, and the odour of bass grazed with lemon. All these smells came together into one smell in its entirety that filled my lungs and sat heavy inside of me. I knew she felt nothing for me because of the way she looked at me. It was the same look she gave everyone. She spoke more with her eyes than with her mouth, and it seemed we had a mutual agreement not to love each other.

The food arrived.

'Do you always do that?' she said.

'What's that?' I said.

'Talk to yourself.'

'Was I talking to myself?'

'Your mouth was moving,' she said. 'And you mumbled something. If you have something to say, say it.'

'I don't have anything to say.'

A couple on the next table had drunk all their wine and asked for some more. I decided to order more wine too. I ordered white wine again. I immediately regretted this decision. I thought wine was disgusting. It tasted of acid, burned my tongue. I watched her drink it. She left red lipstick imprinted on the glass.

'Have you had too much wine, Carl?' she laughed. She was making fun of me.

'It tastes like battery acid,' I said.

Her glass sat empty and drunk, the red lip imprint on it like a rose. Her eyes now completely black and the black of her eyes, enlarged with the wine, just stared at me. It was unsettling, left me with nothing to say. I chewed on a piece of bread and looked over at the couple on the next table who were already halfway through their second bottle. Their grins, ugly upward slits. I looked at Jennifer again and she was still staring. Her slight smile caused creases at the corners of her eyes. She was 35 years old. I was 25.

When we'd finished eating, we both sat back in our chairs, full. I felt a little sick, maybe I'd eaten too much, maybe it was the wine.

She said, 'I hope the waiter comes and clears all this away soon.'

'We're leaving in a bit,' I said.

'I know,' she said. 'But I don't like mess. It's just sitting there between us. I don't want it.'

'Let's not eat, then,' I said.

'I will some other time, just not now,' she said. 'But this wine. We both enjoy it. We both want more.' Again, she stared at me as though she had more to say but didn't want to say it.

'I see.'

'Do you know what I mean?'

'You like the wine better than the food.'

'I suppose,' she said. She crossed her arms. 'Like when my mother was pregnant with my sister. I was only a little girl, but I could read the room like a book. The mess was unbearable, I ended up tidying up after her. It surprised me how messy a pregnant woman can be. It's called nesting. They make a nest.'

'I didn't know that.'

The food sat in front of us, monotone, gunmetal with the depressing dinge of grease and the revolting smell attached to it. I had to push it away so I wouldn't have to smell it anymore. I had, in turn, pushed the plates in front of her when I hadn't meant to, so she began to pile the plates on top of each other, throwing scrunched up napkins on top, collating the cutlery.

23

The waiter came to clear the table. I imagined his surprise at the tidiness, which made me laugh. We decided to order some more drinks before we left. One for the road. This time I ordered a beer.

She said to me, 'Where in the world would you want to be other than here? And who with?'

'Anywhere as long as I'm on my own.'

'Why? Do you hate people?'

'No, I'm just fed up with them.'

'You can't spend all your time alone, even if you want to.'

'Why not?'

'It's too sad.'

'Okay,' I said. 'I'd travel across the American desert. In a car. Like Hunter Thompson. All the drugs I can eat.'

She laughed. 'But who would you take?'

'Do you want to come with me?'

'Okay.'

'Okay, I'll take you with me.'

'I'd go to Prague,' she said. 'I'd go to the beach but only when it's bleak. I love a bleak beach. Like all grey and cloudy and miserable. But not miserable to me because I'd enjoy it.'

'You enjoy it grey and cloudy?' I said, not having the heart to tell her there are no beaches in Prague.

'Yeah. Imagine it. When it's sunny it's annoying. So many people: sunbathing, coloured shorts, sweat and sunscreen. That, to me, is miserable. I'd love a beach to be grey and cloudy. A little bit of rain. Almost silent. The wind. A seagull.'

'Who would you take?'

'No one.'

'Not me?'

'No.'

'Oh.'

'I wonder where our drinks are.'

'Maybe he forgot,' I said.

'How could he forget?' she said. 'It was a simple order.'

'Maybe he forgot about *us*.'

'Only a terrible waiter would forget us.'

'Maybe you're not as memorable as you think.'

'Thanks,' she said, sarcastically.

Soon, the waiter came over and told us that the particular white wine Jennifer wanted was now off the menu. She didn't know what to order, then she changed her mind and she didn't order anything. She stared at me while I drank my beer.

The other couple had gone. They left dirty plates and cutlery, glasses smudged with lipstick, and there was a hot odour of perspiration tinged with perfume that hovered in the space where they had been. I said to Jennifer, 'I don't know what to make of you.'

'What do you mean?'

'I don't know,' I said.

'Please, whatever you do, don't fall in love with me.'

'Why not?'

'I don't want it,' she said. 'And you'd end up changing your mind.'

Once I'd drank my beer, we went outside. It was cold. It had got dark while we were inside which gave the sense that time had broken down and we were the last two awkward souls left in the void. We headed towards the cinema to see a film. She loved films. I'd known her for three years and I knew nothing about her except for the fact that she loved old films. Many I'd never

heard of, even the actors didn't seem real. The cinema was
showing these old films, so I'd asked her to go. It was only a
short walk from the restaurant, but the walk itself was long and
strained with our pained silent gestures.

'It's cold.'

'Yeah.'

I got the tickets for *Double Indemnity*, a film she said she'd
seen a dozen times. We walked upstairs where there was a bar
and a crowd of people. It was warm here. I felt the thick residue
of body heat, a disgusting intimacy of strangers surrounding the
bar. She told me to meet her at the bar while she went to the
ladies to put on her face. That's what she'd said. She was going
to put on her face as if she was going to come out as someone
completely different.

Of course, I felt something for her, but nothing I could
put my finger on. It all ran through my head so quickly that I
couldn't quite grasp what it was I wanted, and it frightened me. I
decided to leave. I walked down the stairs and through the lobby
where people were still buying their *Double Indemnity* tickets. The
warm salt smell of popcorn like the salt smell of the sea.

When I reached the lobby door, I changed my mind.
What the hell was I doing? I couldn't just leave her there. I felt
the chill from the outside as people came in. I turned around
and headed back upstairs where she was. I told her I'd gone to
the toilet. She smiled.

While we sat, waiting for the film to start, I said to her,
'So is this like a black and white film?'

And she said, 'It's *like* a black and white film because it *is*
a black and white film.' She began to rummage in her handbag.
It was difficult to see what she was doing. She merged into the
darkness. She was a shadow. She was my shadow. She took out a

cheese sandwich and ate it as the film began. She made sounds that she was deaf to. I heard the sound of her voice in a cough.

She was a fan of Edward G. Robinson. I didn't know who that was. She showed me him when he was on screen. She told me I looked like him, but I think she was lying because I looked nothing like him. She loved everything about him. The way he spoke. The clothes he wore. He was something to her. Edward G. Robinson meant more to her than I did.

We left. We walked down the road. We walked past a poster for *Jaws*. It was being shown again. She told me she first saw it on VHS when she was five years old and it was a huge part of her life. She loved that film. I said I loved that film too. I wasn't even born when *Jaws* first came out. She had a beautiful face. I smelled the wine on her breath, hot and acidic, but sweet like an apple. She touched my arm as we walked. She touched my arm when other men walked past us, moving closer to me.

'The reason I love films so much is because they aren't real,' she said. 'We're all arseholes in real life. I love *Double Indemnity*, seeing people in the 1940s dress well, wearing hats, and talking with the most perfect wit. Imagine we all spoke as if all our dialogue was written by Raymond Chandler.'

We had a lot in common but I couldn't think of anything to say. The alcohol had subdued me. We said goodbye near a phone box. She smiled and waved to me.

She said, 'See you Wednesday,' and walked away. In this action, I imagined she was watching me on the big screen, as though I was a fictional character in a film; something and nothing to her at the same time.

I walked away. I turned to look, but she was gone.

The Sea Captain

I used to come here with my wife. I'm sixty-seven years old now but I remember her only as a young woman – thirty years ago, maybe, was that the last time I saw her? I retired last month but I won't get much in the way of a pension. I have nothing to do now. The sand is hard and wet beneath my shoes. The sky is white and has turned grey far-off in the distance like a giant smudge from a HB pencil. The cold white sun glows behind the clouds letting off a strong light which makes the ground I walk on look like gold.

Arthur McNally died. I'm older than he was when I first met him. He must have been getting on a bit. Arthur took care of me when I started working at Rich & John's Hardware. That's where I learnt everything there is to know about spanners and screws and steel and aluminium. He made me a cup of tea on my first day, sweeter than sugar and hotter than the sun, and we watched John Hartington batter a piece of steel with a flatter hammer, the sharp acidic aroma coming from the beaten sheet of metal smelled like a thunderstorm. I didn't go to his funeral. I hadn't seen him in so long that I no longer knew who he was. He's just a name now. I had a call from Lucy Jackson who had started working there just before I left. She said, 'Arthur died. Sorry. I got your number off John. Didn't think it'd still be the right number, but there we go.' I asked her how he died but she didn't know. 'I thought you'd like to know. You two were friends, weren't you?' I didn't know if that was a question. I couldn't see her face to read her expression to understand it, but I also didn't know the answer if it *was* a question. Were we friends? He was much older than I was. He must have been as old as I am now. But we did enjoy each other's company. We must have been friends. How could I have not known until now?

The beach is cold and quiet and a harsh downpour on the ridges of the Welsh mountains far-off, covered in crystallised rain, the pale haze of a slow-moving fog, gives the sensation my eyes are blurry. Someone told me about those mountains when I was younger, that King Arthur was buried there, but I never really understood the fascination with him – but now it's my Arthur who has died. I wonder if they'd bury him over there with his namesake king.

The further I walk, the more the sand becomes firmer and wetter. It's noisier too, the roar of the waves, though gentle here compared to where they were further out at sea. They clap and splash against each other and quickly roll up the sand close to me. There are small footprints in the sand leading towards the water. I follow them until I can see the old dock.

Many years ago, when I was thirteen, when I was a little further up the beach at the docks, I met someone. It was a warm day and the salt stink rose in the muscular air between the two quays overflowing with busy people, and they all seemed to know what to do, communicating by yelling across the quay or dropping a crate for someone else to collect. They all worked together, synchronised like dancers. An acidic waft of fish, strong in the air, and their watery dead eyes under snowy patches of ice. I walked to the far end where the reefer ship was, where the stink of something rotten sat stagnant and brought up the hot bile in my throat. It was like a wall of warm infected breath. The air got warmer and warmer and even the harsh vinegar of the men's odour didn't overpower the smell of the stinking ship.

I remember when the reefer ship pulled in, the sulphuric twang of noxious old farts and sweat seeping out of the cracks as it unloaded its cargo, relieving the men onboard who had been at sea for several weeks and needed to ground their sea legs. This ship was much dirtier than the others. It looked as dirty as it smelt. The stink, the putrid decomposing something in there, along with the black and green grime under the wooden beams like dirt underneath fingernails. That's the reason I remember that ship. I couldn't tell you a thing about any other ship if they were clean and tidy. They were unmemorable. This one though, I remembered it so well I could have been onboard.

Along the quayside there was a fence surrounding the perimeter of the docks which, on the other side of the border, was where my mother and I lived, but on this side it was another world. Giant giraffe-necked cranes reached up towards the sky, parting the clouds with their small heads. You could see these cranes for miles, as far as Wales on a clear day. I'd walked without getting caught through this concrete and steel section of the world and was fascinated by this dirty old ship. The smell made me feel sick in my stomach. It smelled of rotten meat, as horrible and pungent as sweat. One by one the seafarers came out and I watched them get to work, lugging things from the deck, the crane screeching overhead to lift the crates over to the quayside.

At the port side (I'd learnt that term from school) was a tall wide-chested man with long legs and long arms, one of which bent up to a hand stroking a white beard. He was the captain, I guessed from his uniform. Everyone seemed to be busy except for him. I walked towards him. He looked as if he was in deep thought, a deep deathly look I hadn't seen in anyone's eyes before. His brow was drawn down heavily causing wrinkles in the image of crashing waves; the lines coursed down in small canals past his eyes. The pores in his skin, wide and filthy, covered his nose in little black dots.

'What do you have in your ship?' I asked him, my boyish voice like a slight wind among the low tones of masculine speech.

The sea captain seemed startled as if from a deep sleep. He looked down at me and dropped his hand from his beard. 'Food,' he said. 'We got tons of beef carcasses hanging in there. Perishable goods. But, as you can tell from the smell, some did perish.'

'What happened?'

'Well, about fifteen days ago we lost power to the refrigeration unit. There's a lot of rotten beef in there. I don't know about you but seeing a cow decompose in front of you day after day really does something to a man…'

The sea captain trailed off, again looking out at the distance, a blank look in his eyes.

'I've never been out at sea before,' I said. My voice was carried off with the wind and stink, the male noises, shouting, banging, clanging, the aggressive churn of the crane's engine. Three men came down from the ship and weakly saluted the captain who didn't even see them. It was like his thoughts passed blankly as a cold wind in a far-off place that no one would ever feel or know. On board that ship for weeks, floating in an otherworldly place, no land in sight as though they would never see land again, swallowed up whole by this gargantuan oceanic beast rising fifty feet in the air, crashing down on them, rain, rain, and more rain in the bitter cold and dark forever.

'Where've you come from?'

'Massachusetts,' the sea captain said. 'Port of Boston. Set off from there twenty days ago. Would have been here sooner if not for the storm.'

'There was a storm?' I said.

'Aye,' said the captain. 'Nearly killed the lot of us.'

'You're American then?' I said. 'You don't sound American.'

'I'm not American,' he said.

'Where are you from?'

The sea captain turned away from me for the first time since our interaction began. He said something else but it probably wasn't the answer to my question as he seemed to speak to one of the crew. His voice was accentless. He didn't seem to have any specific place about him as though he was birthed in the vast salty amniotic ocean. Were he to acknowledge me, he would have had to reveal something about himself which he wasn't willing to do, not for anyone, let alone a small boy from a city where he'd just arrived. The old sea captain looked extremely tired. His eyes didn't look kind but they didn't look hostile either. It was as though he was a statue of a man, frozen in time.

'These are seafaring men,' the captain said to me. 'They know nothing except the job they do. While on land they'll finish up, have some time off, then get back on the sea where they belong.'

'Sea fearing men.'

'Faring,' he said. 'Seafaring men. They belong on the sea.'

I leant my hands on a short black bollard where thick rope and chains were wrapped around. I peered over the edge at the water where the massive hull of the ship was floating, the bow like a knife that cut into the soft tissue of the water. As I peered over, the backwards letters of the ship reflected, and there, my tiny head, so small I hardly recognised myself. This was like looking up at the stars in space and feeling so small, though this wasn't the ocean, it was just a small bit of water between the quayside and the ship. The idea of the vast ocean frightened me then. The ocean, to the captain, was far greater than the blackness of space. The sun and stars had no place in the waters below. Nothing went down there that didn't belong. The blackest part of the ocean bed was much worse than the deepest, coldest parts of space.

'Your parents take you to church, lad?'

'My mum goes,' I said. 'I go.'

'If you've read the Bible then you get the idea of God. But with the sea, you don't have to believe it because it's there. The sea's much bigger than any god.'

The sea captain was soon taken away with his duties and disappeared up the ramp onto the ship's deck. I felt stupid to have expected a goodbye or a wave, even a smile, but there was nothing. I just watched him, white beard, smart captain's suit, vanish out of my line of sight. Men began yelling and not long after, the ship had moved off and another ship was coming in to dock. Soon the awful smell of rotten meat was gone and all that was left was oil and petrol and the distant yet flavoursome taste of salt in the air.

I get as far as the beach will let me before the rocks block my path, but where I'd be able to see the docks back then. There's nothing here anymore. Just some cranes and crates, all fenced off and secure. It's a shame, really, looking at it now, all industry without charm. The ghosts of the old dock moaning in the wind, the ghosts of the dockers and the seafaring men. The

wind gets up. Water lapping at the rocks, fizzing and frothing. I
never saw that same stinking reefer ship again.

*

A downpour came in from the Welsh mountains and settled in
the sea bringing in a cold draught. On the horizon, several wind
turbines were positioned in the sea but the grey mist obscured
them and made them into whirling dervishes. After the day I met
the sea captain, my family broke apart; my parents divorced, my
sister married and moved to another country, all my
grandparents died one after the other and by the time I was a
grown man I found that the concept of family was merely a
word. That said, I did try when I met Hannah. We had a son,
Oscar. We moved around a lot with her job as a make-up artist,
as she worked for film studios, which paid very well. And I was
happy with my life, spending most of my time with Oscar and
seeing which actors and actresses on TV were the one's Hannah
had worked on. But I never forgot that man. The captain.
Though, it did occur to me that it might have not been real.
Maybe the whole thing was a made-up memory. The mind does
that sometimes, doesn't it? Made-up like the way my wife made-
up beautiful faces for TV and film.

Our home was a modest little house not far from the
coast, near a few shops and the train station. The plants around
the front made it look nicer than it really was; the gutters were in
disrepair, a few clay roof tiles were missing from the storm last
winter, and the boiler was about to kick it in. I thought I'd be
happy to be away from this house.

Inside it was already empty and white as the inside of an
abandoned hermit crab shell. My voice echoed against the walls,

34

hard and tinny as if I was hearing the ghost voice of my teenage self, awkward and alone, pleading for something new out of the aether. There were cardboard boxes filled to bursting, pregnant with old used-up memories, and suitcases, and our diningware bubble wrapped and taped up, left to one side.

Hannah was stuffing the final suitcase with clothes as if she was about to go on holiday. She was red in the face, forehead damp, some hair stuck to the skin above her eyes. 'Come get this,' she said. 'Can you take over with it? It's just Oscar's clothes left now.' She walked as if in a rush to the other side of the room and picked up the bubble wrapped plates and placed them into a box on the table. Hannah and I, a year after we met, got a mortgage on the house just before Oscar was born. I couldn't imagine not being there. It was my anchor to life, and now we were moving away from it, taking with us bubble wrapped and boxed memories, kidding ourselves we could take some of that life with us.

'Where did you go?' she asked me.

'The beach,' I said. 'One last walk around.'

'Are you okay?'

I paused. Then I said, 'I'm not going to like it.'

'You said yourself there's nothing here for you. I don't know why you're getting upset. I'm sorry, I do care that you feel this way, but I'd prefer if you got upset about things that mattered. You always get upset about things that don't matter.'

'Well I'm upset, aren't I,' I said. I heard my voice rising, banging almost off the solid, bare walls.

'And what about Oscar?' she said. But this wasn't even a question. There was no answer to it. She did that. She'd say 'what about this?' 'what about that?' as if I could pull an answer out of thin air and everything would be okay. But since Oscar was born she liked using that one. 'What about Oscar?' As if our son was the end all and be all. And he was. Because his name, like a religious invocation, ended the argument.

I packed the suitcase full of Oscar's clothes, zipped it up and dragged it over to the door where the rest of the stuff was.

'It's raining,' she said.

'Yeah, I saw it coming in.'

'Won't see it coming in when we're in London,' she said.

We drove down. The six-hour trip, in my mind, went by quickly. When we arrived, I began unpacking straight away, setting up the home, even refusing a glass of wine from Hannah because I didn't want to stop. Got the clothes out, put them in drawers, hung up pictures, filled the kitchen with food. Most of the furniture had already been sent down before us, some furniture was already there in the purchase price anyway. I thought some of the rooms needed painting, but that's when I stopped, the wine shoved in my hand, at midnight, drank it, tasted its blood-tang, drank half the bottle, fell asleep. I remember that first day. Oscar wouldn't even remember Liverpool.

I was extremely proud of Hannah's success as a make-up artist. Once when we went to the cinema, she pointed out Kate Winslet when she was on-screen, saying, 'I did that. Look at her eyes. Oh my god, she's beautiful.' Someone shushed us, but I could tell she didn't care. Before we moved to London, Hannah had to move around with work, and I either stayed at home with Oscar or sometimes we came with her. Now she didn't have to move around, but it still meant I stayed put with Oscar in our two-bedroom flat. That first year was fine. I enjoyed spending time with him. I took him to the park, letting him walk with me hand-in-hand, letting him run across the grass. He sat with me in cafés as I drank coffee and read. It just felt like a trip to London. The impermanence of it made me indifferent to the environment in which I was in, made me unfazed by the monolithic buildings and the hustle and bustle of the capital.

When I bathed him, his small round shoulders slouched allowing the notches of his spine to appear in his back. I poured the water over his head to rinse the shampoo out of his hair turning it as black as his mother's. Soon, he started school and I became so incredibly lonely that I didn't know what to do with myself.

Hannah's job soon took her away from me again. There was a new production which was being filmed over in Ireland, and Hannah had to go, especially now she was a senior member of staff. I wished her luck and kissed her goodbye, knowing I'd see her again in a couple of weeks. It was just the thought of being in that flat by myself. Bored to death.

I began to read a lot. I read Beckett going mad, Ishiguro becoming robotic, Melville obsessed. Creased and torn up books lay scattered around the living room. I read them as though eating them; chewing them with my eyes, digesting them in my brain, shitting them out in my thoughts and dreams. In the bath, I read and drifted off into restless sleeps. I began dreaming recurringly that I was lost at sea, naked, in the water, and I was terrified a shark would bite off my penis. The sky was always gunmetal grey, blackening like soot against the misty horizon where rain sprayed in violent torrents. I was always away from the storm; I never knew if it was coming towards me or going away from me. The first time I dreamt one of these dreams I woke up as my nose sunk below water level. I started, quite violently, but indignant against myself I kept my head underwater, away from the dry pages of my books and into the glorious suffocating world beneath. I envied it. I wanted to envelop myself in the greenish murky water, soapy and stinking. I resigned myself to this, breathed in, and choked. Again, my body violently jerked upwards, coughing and gagging, vomiting almost from the water in my lungs and the taste of my own bathwater. Afterwards I sulked on the bed, wearing nothing but a towel. Later, I went out to collect Oscar from school.

The car was uncomfortably hot. Sweat trickled from my armpits beneath my clothes and I was becoming self-conscious of sweat patches on my t-shirt and the smell my body was giving off. The sun was just a giant white orb – I was wearing sunglasses – and I imagined a spotlight for the actors who were wearing Hannah's make-up. Their famous faces created by my wife. If I was on the spotlight now, beneath the heat of that giant halogen bulb, I wondered what I'd look like. How beautiful would she make me?

I waited a few minutes in the sweltering heat, whimpering like a dog, impatient and anxious. I wanted to get back home, take a bath and read. I waited god-knows how long, maybe the heat was getting to me, and I thought for a moment if I was too early. Then a crowd of children came crashing out of the front door and I saw Oscar within the crowd, pushing through the surging waves of screaming faces. He walked alongside a woman. She had long, straight brown hair, as plain as a primary school teacher could be. There was nothing special about her. Not even the awkward gait in the way she walked or the way she held onto her arm as though for comfort but at the same time looking like a wounded soldier. She came over to the car and Oscar jumped in the back where he liked to sit. Miss

Singer, her name was – Alice Singer – placed her two small hands on the frame of the opened window and said, 'Mister Brown?'

'Edward,' I said.

'Edward,' she said. 'Do you have a minute? I'd to talk to you about Oscar.'

'Yeah, not a problem,' I said.

'Is that a Liverpool accent?' she said.

'It is,' I said. 'We moved here a few months ago.'

'I was sure I could hear that in Oscar's voice,' she said. 'Sounds like his old accent is fading away. Well, I hope you like it here. But I'm afraid to say, Oscar has been quite disruptive in class today. It's unfortunate because it's not like him at all. I thought it best to run it by you because I hope he's doing well at home.'

'That's unlike you, Oscar,' I called to the back seat. I caught his small, passive face in the rear-view mirror, uninterested and bored. He didn't look like he'd been trouble today. He acted as though nothing was wrong. 'I'm sorry, Miss Singer, it is unlike him. I don't know what's got into him.'

'Alice,' she said. 'Well, he was bothering the other pupils, running around and not listening to me. I had a hard time calming him down. When I did, he kicked Mrs Wheeler in the shin. She's our teaching assistant. She wasn't too happy about it.'

'My mother told me I was like that when I was his age,' I said. 'She wouldn't let me hear the end of it. Apparently, I used to wander off and bother people. I suppose it's difficult when another generation is a handful as well.'

'Well, he seems to have calmed down now.'

'Yeah, he seems pretty calm now,' I said. 'Well done.'

She smiled, lifted her hands from the car window frame. 'I'll have a word with him when we get home,' I said. She smiled again and said goodbye to us both. I watched her walk back to the school as the many children dispersed and soon the schoolgrounds became quiet and still. It became quiet very quickly as though none of that had just happened. It occurred to me that only half an hour ago I'd almost died in the bath. I imagined the water again, that bitter, cloudy nothingness.

Oscar liked to keep to himself, so you'd forget he was even there, sat in front of the TV. I wanted a beer but I decided to have a cup of coffee instead. It was hot and earthy, the soil of the granules as bitter as salt. I spat it out. Had I put salt in it instead of sugar? What was I thinking? I poured it into the sink – I changed my mind about having a coffee or a beer – and went and sat with Oscar in front of the TV. I didn't say anything to him and he didn't say anything to me. I never really saw myself as a father and Oscar seemed like a boy who'd wandered in off the street. It sounds terrible, but it was because we never spoke. I don't think I really knew *who* he was. I looked at him, half-expecting to see one of the other kids from the school. I put him to bed an hour later and I stayed up watching a film until I fell asleep.

I saw Alice Singer again when I was picking Oscar up from school. Her eyes, looking at me, were a kind of hazelnut. Her pupils as black as coffee. We often talked while Oscar sat bored in the back seat of the car. I began to see her on weekends or on evenings when I went to the pub for a beer.

Hannah had to stay over in Ireland for several more weeks because the production of the film had somehow been delayed. Over the phone, she was both excited and disappointed. I understood, though. She loved her job. She spoke with Oscar over the phone, and when I took the phone back she told me to give her love to him and that she loved me too.

*

A year later, Hannah, Oscar and I were living comfortably in our flat. I got used to London and I'd made friends with a few people on our street. It was Oscar's eighth birthday and we were going out for something to eat. It was the middle of summer. August. The sun was glaring and white and the old streets of Bayswater were filled with people going this way and that.

I didn't think the meal would last long since I doubted Oscar would be too pleased about having to sit still in a restaurant for an hour or so. But Hannah thought it would be a nice thing to do. Across the restaurant, Alice Singer was there with a woman – I learnt was her sister – and a baby. She'd been on maternity leave and I hadn't seen her in some time. I only noticed her because the baby kept on crying and crying. Its loud, tinny whining sounded like a bird trapped in the rafters. We seemed to see each other at the same time and I smiled. She got up in a fluster, red-faced and with a strange kind of embarrassment forced upon herself; I thought that she needn't get up just for me, since a simple smile would have done, but she came over, baby in arms. I introduced Hannah to her, Oscar's teacher, but without warning she plopped the screaming baby into my lap, saying, 'There, that's yours. You deal with it now.' She then looked between Hannah and Oscar and said, in a quieter tone, 'Sorry for ruining your evening.'

The boy was mine. This tiny, plump raisin-wrinkled thing the weight of a bag of flour sat in my lap, wailing like a creature from a Lynchian nightmare. Although, the top of his

41

head smelled wonderful – like Oscar's did when he was a baby and I was reminded of the first few days of his life when I felt like I was born into something new as well, a different man entirely – I knew this was the end of my marriage. That was Oscar's memorable eighth birthday. Memorable for me, though I hoped he'd quickly forget it and remember some of his good ones. Alice walked off, leaving the restaurant, but the other woman, who was Alice's sister, came over with an apologetic face – though I could see her allyship with her sister probably meant she thought I'd deserved it – and took the baby and left as well. Hannah, without speaking, took Oscar and left the restaurant, and I was left there alone. I paid the bill and left.

Hannah divorced me and took Oscar away. Alice moved to the Welsh coast. The following month proved difficult in what I had to decide to do. I only had my packed bags and my car. Nothing else. It seemed like I had no choice. I could have chosen nothing or chosen to deal with my mistake. I drove to where Alice was – she was still in contact with me after she moved – and although she didn't want anything to do with me, she'd said I was allowed to see Ewan. Our son.

Ewan was a toddler by this time, so I'd let him walk beside me on the beach. He was quick with that awkward child's gait, and he liked the water. He loved running towards it, fascinated by it. It was always something new to him, this white-silver current rushing in and pulling itself back, luring with a sense of urgency. As the tide came in, kissed at his feet, cold and strange, he'd scream, dance a little, and run back to me. I thought he was charming, and I enjoyed being with him. His mop of coffee-brown hair, like his mother's, blew about him in the seaside air. Often, I'd look up the coastline, north, and think about home – my original home. I wondered what it was like there without me all this time. Though, it sort of felt like, standing on the sand, that I *was* there in a way, if I imagined it was just one long beach stretching up the Welsh coast, meeting England at the breast. I spent several afternoons with Ewan on the beach, but it wouldn't last since I didn't have much money. All the time I'd spent with Hannah, she'd paid for almost everything, and I was happy to stay at home, looking after Oscar. But Alice, having took up another job at a primary school not far from Aberystwyth, was relying on me to help pay the bills. I did try. I worked at Rich & John's Hardware. I lived in a house-share and saw Ewan on Sundays. Soon, my job, Alice and Ewan made me forget about Hannah and Oscar and London. That's just how the mind works. It moves on.

I never spoke to Hannah and again and I found out, as Oscar grew up, that he didn't even want to know me anymore. I was dead to him. I suppose I didn't deserve either of them, and that was my fault entirely. I'd lost control of the direction my life was going, and all of a sudden I was somewhere else. Ewan enjoyed my company and I enjoyed his. It was a strange relationship. This boy, immaculate in a way (but not quite), seeming to appear in my life out of thin air. Who was he? I could have asked, but I tried to see him as my son and not just some boy.

Rich & John's Hardware was situated not far from the beach so I had a nice, easy walk to the promenade when I clocked off in the evening. This was when I met Arthur McNally. A sixty year-old socialist who told me stories of his exploits when he was younger when he'd picket outside the docks over pay disputes. He wouldn't get paid for weeks. His family almost starved, all in the name of fairness. But what was fair? Life surely wasn't. He lived a different life to me, a different world. He knew the power one man can have over the collective, and how that group can work together as one. Communicating and working together somehow, synchronised and coordinated.

Arthur showed me how to hit a piece of metal with a flatter hammer, bringing it down with his long, powerful arms. He showed me how to accurately cut furniture joinery with a tenon saw. Rich & John's sold tools and equipment, but they also offered blacksmithing and joinery services. The people that worked there were skilled tradesmen, and Arthur, a carpenter by trade before he worked there, showed me a lot of what he knew.

'You're like Jesus, aren't you?' I said, joking with him. 'The carpenter.'

'I'm not sure about that,' he said, scratching his beard. 'You a churchgoer?'

'No,' I said. 'It was just a joke.'

'I was raised Catholic,' he said. 'I took up the bloody trade of Christ.' He laughed, dragging the saw back and forth as it aggressively tore through the wood as if through water.

When my mother died, Arthur was the only one I told. A friend of my mother had called Hannah, but the message was passed to me from one of my old neighbours in London. Arthur asked about my father but I didn't have an answer for him.

I enjoyed those years of my life. I particularly enjoyed being with Ewan, taking him down to the beach and telling him my stories of the sea captain. How I saw him once as a little boy and how his ship stunk and how he boarded the ship again with his crew and sailed off into the great wide ocean. There were other stories too. How the sea captain sailed through a torrential storm in the middle of the Pacific, over a wave fifty feet high. How he and his crew docked in America and saw bears and wolves, animals you never see over here. How he vowed to return again, this time with good fresh beef. I could see he was fascinated with these stories, most I made up from the top of my head just to entertain him, watching his eyes light up as he imagined this mystical man in a far-off land.

It was a Sunday and I had been with Ewan on the beach, letting him run barefoot towards the rushing water and back again, leaving small footprints in the sand. He wanted to get closer to the water, fascinated with it now because of the stories of the sea captain. The sea captain in my mind then, mystified by the endless sea, the darkened sky, the greenish, metallic colour of the far-off water. It was always somewhere I hadn't been. Somewhere I'd never be.

He just wanted to get a little closer. I'd been with him and then I wasn't. The boy had wandered off into the sea. My heart seemed to stop. Everything seemed to stop.

*

I follow the footprints in the sand as far as my old knees will allow me to go, but they don't lead to anything; the tide rushes in, washing away any markings that anyone was ever there. I just wanted to be alone today, thinking about Arthur. But that got me thinking about everything else. I feel the pull on my beard as the wind blows, though the sea is calm today. I've never been out at sea before.

Look at it. It's like someone you never really got to know. The salt air is harsh on my bones; my knees feel like they could give way. I'm sure if I cough into a tissue, only salt would come out.

Remember the Lake

We remember the house we grew up in and its totem pole washing line leaning to one side in the back yard like a dead tree, rust-brown and oily, the orange flakes coming off on your hand when Mum yells not to touch it. We remember the concrete and little sprouting shoots of grass like what she fed us on a Sunday with the overcooked chicken. The soot-black bricks as if the house always wanted it to be night as I pretended to be asleep while my brother snored in the bed next to me, and I'd look out the window at the black and silver world, the crooked washing line, wet concrete and grass.

'Come on then, if you're coming,' I'd hear most mornings. My dad and his brother – Uncle Robert – stinking of the flesh of outdoors, a cold smell like sour milk covered in what my brother said was Old Spice, which I thought was another thing to put on your Sunday roast. I remember their boots; big, hefty things like boulders, the black of the rubber soles like the gums of a dog, dried mud, laces fastened only once with impossibly tight knots, scratches and scuffs exposing a history long before me.

My brother, Matthew, loved going fishing. He'd be ready before I was. I got washed in the sink, the gold shine of sun through the frosted glass, shining on me; I remember how I looked, thin face, skin like paper not yet written on. I brushed my yellow baby teeth. Got dressed. I didn't have boots, just a pair of dirty trainers, the scuffs in the rubber like the first few wrinkles in an aging face.

I remember the lake. Matthew, my dad, and Uncle Robert. I remember the cold, but I also remember how the cold *looked.* Like a bright glare from a cold fat sun through a thin mist between hard bare branches. I could see my breath. I watched my dad's breath. A white cloud. There and gone. There and gone.

My uncle leaned back, holding the line, tight as piano wire, that pulled the fish from beneath the water. My dad helped him, grabbing his brother's forearms and yanking against the weight of the fish. His arms filled with many cords and wires. His sunburnt skin covered in a light blonde fur. Matthew and I just watched them pulling the line, almost expecting a marionette puppet to come dancing out of the lake, but eventually this huge fish emerged, jelly-like, mouth open in a wide O, black wet pebble eyes. The silver green trout flopped on its side, the slime caught in the shining sun, glowing, this heavy thing, like a baby, frantically breathing, and the stink, a vinegar and salt smell clung to my clothes forever hanging on the bent washing line left out to dry. I held it in my hands. It was cold and heavy. Thick like muscle. My uncle patted me on the shoulder and it felt like it was me who'd caught the fish, as though my brother and I were the two grown men fishing in the lake that cold morning. Everything looked bright. In my memory, anyway. The sun must have caught in the lake. My dad's face and my uncles face burned into the retina of my mind.

I stopped hearing that voice in the morning calling me to get a move on. My dad developed a sadness with Uncle Robert not being around anymore and the fishing trips became fewer and fewer. Dark patterns formed under Dad's eyes and in the corners of his mouth, which was wide and drooped down like the mouth of a fish. He took up a second job when my sister was born and it was as though he was so tired he refused to talk to me or my brother anymore. You forget things. You forget the fishing trips and you forget the people around you.

One night I stayed awake and looked out the window. It was quiet and the night was black. If I stood there long enough, I'd see the cats begin fighting over who got to sit on the corner of the fence. Their fur up in fluffy plumes, screaming at each other like children. I woke up Matthew and his hair was sticking up like the cat's fur and it made me laugh. We sat on the windowsill for a few hours watching the cats scream at each other until we both fell asleep. We dreamt of the lake. I don't know why.

I began to lose my sight in my mid-thirties. Had to wear glasses to correct my vision, at first just for reading and then to help me to see. The world was a blur without them. My glasses were the first thing my wife, Charlotte, noticed about me – before we were married. 'Like Coke bottles,' she said, laughing, her teeth white polished marble, her eyes wet and almost black. Six years after we met, Luke was born. As a baby he had a habit of taking my glasses off my face, and each time he turned into an indistinct blur, shapeless; it became impossible to form new memories.

'I won't be able to see you anymore, you know,' I said. 'What have I got if I can't even see you or Luke?'

'You don't need your eyes to see,' she said. Her mouth moved in slow-quick rhythms like waves in water.

The lake was smaller than I remembered. The branches still bare, balding with the age of winter, the cold chill underneath my clothes, in my bones. I didn't see much colour, there never was much colour that time of year, but my eyes didn't recognise how the world looked anymore. The place was like a drawing; I could have drawn it myself and stepped into it to remind myself how it all looked. There was something on the water, I thought maybe it was a boat. I squinted but couldn't quite see it.

We remember the house we grew up in –

Every so often I remember everything, but the world became so different. Matthew put on a lot of weight, short, stubby, but dressed well with shirt and tie. Hair combed and neat. I recognised his eyes. My sister, too, with a thin face like Dad, stood shyly at the kitchen window holding her arms across her body into a mangled shape of a cross.

'Don't you remember when we went fishing?' I said.

'I never went,' my sister said. 'I was too young, and then you all just stopped going.'

I looked out the window. The washing line was gone by this point; there was just a little rusty stub sticking out the ground like a bone. The house was stripped bare of all memory making our voices echo against the hard blank walls. The sign out front – FOR SALE.

'There's a lot of memories in this place,' I said. 'A shame to see it go.'

'More memories on that lake,' Matthew said.

'I don't know why you haven't taken Luke there yet,' my sister said. 'I'm sure he'll love it there.'

'No,' I said. 'I wouldn't be much use on a boat these days,' I said. 'I think I'll be blind by next summer.'

'There's more to it than just looking at the place,' Matthew said.

I thought about it. I thought about the times we had, fishing on that lake. I thought that, years later, I'll take Luke fishing. Charlotte will join us. The smells and sounds all very familiar, and Luke's voice sometimes sounding like Matthew's voice at that age. The sounds of water, of birds, of Charlotte's voice, Luke yelling in delight at catching a fish, and I'll feel the thudding of its strange thick body bashing itself against the wooden floor of the boat. I'll ask him to describe it to me and he'll try and I'll laugh. The vinegar and salt stink, water sloshing, bubbling. Trees whispering on the bank. We'll remember this and he'll remember more after me. The silver salt tang running along the sides of my tongue from the fish flapping about in the boat, and my son laughing and laughing and laughing, and Charlotte laughing and laughing, and I won't know anything else but those sounds.

Let's All Be There

She stands in the hallway calling the name 'George' in the middle of the night in a pink dressing gown, holding a tumbler of wine. She walks back into the room and drinks the wine in the tumbler and pours some more. She sits on the bed. There is the not-unpleasant aroma of sleep. She tries but fails to place the glass gently on the floor but it slips from her fingers and clinks on the rug. George comes back. He walks in, leaving the door open. He stands there and stares at her because he's both angry at her and in love with her, for some reason, so he loosens his tie and switches on the television and sits next to her and they watch a film called *The 39 Steps* and George thinks it's a Hitchcock film but he's not sure. He leans against her. They stare forward. The silver static glow makes them look holy and they now act as if the other isn't there.

She changes the channel with the remote. The tendons of her thumb stick out sharply like a credit card beneath the skin. She goes through several channels until George grabs her hand and she stops and leaves a foreign thing on, they both don't know what it is, it doesn't matter.

The television says, 'Je ne sais quoi.'

'What does that mean?' she asks.

'I don't know. What?'

'I don't know either.'

'I thought you knew French.'

'I didn't know this was French.'

George stands and looks at her. Her hands, now sunk to her lap, hold on to each other. He picks up her glass and finds another and pours wine into them. To him, wine is sour and not

51

worth the trouble. The sounds of French words fill the room like the nocturnal noise of the radiator. George's hands are shaking as he brings the glasses over to the bed. He sits down and gives her a glass. She is expressionless. They both drink wine out of glass tumblers watching the French film. Neither of them take their eyes off the television. They are lit up, holy. She takes off the dressing gown and puts on an expensive grey merino wool sweater. As George changes the channel back to *The 39 Steps* he spills wine on her expensive grey merino wool sweater.

'I wish you hadn't done that,' she says, looking at him with a look of disgust in her eyes and she sighs dramatically and gets up and wipes her expensive grey merino wool sweater with a damp cloth and George looks at her, standing in the dark, wiping the wine stain and thinks how much he dislikes wine because it's sour and not worth the trouble but still he always seems to drink it, always goes back to it, always with the hangover the next morning.

'I didn't mean to,' George says. 'I was changing the channel.'

'You've ruined my sweater.'

'It's not ruined.'

'It's ruined.'

Robert Donat on the television says, 'I know what it is to feel lonely.' George now feels like walking out again. He wishes he hadn't come back. But he knows if he does leave she'll call him back and he'll come back and they'll sit on the bed, and drink, and watch TV and sleep and the days'll drift by and he'll think of her and he'll think of himself and he'll have none of the answers.

She sits back down next to him. He feels the heat of her. The dampness on her stomach now like a hole where a pregnancy would be. They're both tired. They drop the empty glasses on the floor, they roll and clink against each other and they both lay there, empty and smelling of wine. She falls asleep first, lying next to him, on her side, young-looking and now less confused. Her hair, blonde and clean, sprawled over her like a blanket. He imagines she doesn't know who he is. She doesn't know anyone; she is asleep to the world. The film ends and something else comes on. He stares blankly at the screen and the light hurts his eyes. He stares off into the dark and feels tired. The TV says, 'Let's all be there,' and he wonders what it means.

'Where?' he asks the television.

The television doesn't reply but instead goes on a break and there is a shampoo advert and George gets up and leaves.

George stands in the hallway and expects to hear his name being called behind him but this time he doesn't hear it because she is asleep. He walks outside and the night is quiet. He gets in his car and drives away.

Green Eyes

The café was so loud Connor couldn't hear a word Rachel was saying. Her mouth moved rhythmically like a performance, like someone speaking in a silent film. She was talking about her brother. Her voice had the same unpieced detachment of being underwater and her eyes kept looking away, distracted. As she looked away again, Connor, too, looked away, looked at the people around him and smelled the dark, rich aroma in the air.

He wanted it to be quiet so he could hear what she was saying. He wanted to be left with her in this hot earthy smell that circled the room like a river. The coffee. It was a comfort to him, always had been, which was why he now wanted Rachel to drink some. Behind the counter, the long metal arm screeched and poured coffee into white mugs behind a wall of steam.

Rachel's head hung down. Her hair hung like rope. Her hair was longer than usual, he thought. But so was his.

'You think I should get a haircut?' he asked.

She looked up. Her eyes were wide as though she'd just woken up from a dream and had forgotten where she was. 'No,' she said. 'No, don't get a haircut. I like your hair like that.'

'You like it like this? But it's a mess.'

'It's nice. Leave it as it is. I don't like you when your hair is short.'

'Oh, thanks.'

'Well, when it's too short you don't look like you.'

'Your hair's getting long,' he said. 'I like it. It looks pretty.'

'No, I want a haircut.'

The waitress came over. She said, 'What can I get you?'

'Two cappuccinos,' Connor said. 'Thank you.'

The waitress smiled at Rachel, wrote something down in her tiny notebook and walked away.

'Why did you say that?' Rachel said.

'Why did I say what?'

'You were rude.'

'I wasn't rude.'

'It was rude.'

'We've been sitting here for five minutes,' he said. 'Why did it take her so long to come over?'

They looked at the waitress who was now behind the counter. She tore the page from her tiny notebook and gave it to another girl. She then went to another table, almost seeming to float as though there was no ground beneath her feet. She didn't smile.

'You see that?' Rachel said.

'What?'

'Look how sad she is.'

'So what?' Connor said. 'I don't know her.'

'Well, you don't know anyone,' she said. 'You don't know me.'

'I know you.'

She stared at him, not speaking.

'Rach. Rachel. Speak to me.'

'No,' she said. 'I'm not speaking.'

'Oh, okay then.'

'Don't talk to me.'

'Please.'

'Just … shut up. Please, just stop talking.'

'But –'

'– Ah.' She pressed the heels of her hands to her eyes.

'What are you doing?'

'If you know me so well, what colour are my eyes?'

'This is stupid. I know what colour your eyes are.'

'Tell me.'

The waitress came back carrying the cappuccinos on a tray. She looked at Rachel who had her hands over her eyes, looked once at Connor, then placed the coffees down on the table. 'There's sugar over by the counter if you want it,' she said.

'Thank you,' Rachel said, her eyes still covered.

The waitress walked away.

'Rachel, please,' Connor began but he paused. He looked at Rachel, looked at her hands covering her eyes and wondered what colour her eyes were. It was hard to think of her eye colour. He saw it every day but now he couldn't for the life of him think what colour they were. Blue, green, brown? Were there other colours? Different shades? How could he not know her eye colour? All those times he'd looked into her eyes, he hadn't really been looking at all.

'Drink your coffee,' he said.

She put down her hands, kept her eyes closed, picked up her coffee, guided it to her mouth, and drank.

'So, you're blind now?' he said. 'You can't see?'

'I don't want to see you, Connor. I don't want to look at you.'

'Why not?'

'You know why.'

The delicate way she lifted the mug to her mouth with both hands was very elegant. With her eyes closed as well, she looked like a shop window mannequin, and even the harsh fluorescent lights above made her waxen almost, the light catching over her arms and her black dress.

Connor shuffled in his seat, looked around to see if anyone was looking at them. No one was. He loosened his tie and pulled at his collar to air his neck.

'I know the colour of your eyes,' he said. 'They're kind of the same colour as the waitress'.'

'The waitress?'

'I think so, yeah.'

'Are you fucking her?'

'The waitress?'

She opened her eyes. 'Are you fucking her?'

'Green.'

'What?'

'Your eyes are green.'

But she was crying. Her eyes were like two wet leaves that had stayed damp from a rain that had long since ended. She drank her coffee. Once the mug hit the wood of the table, Connor decided to speak.

'No, I'm not,' he said. 'I've never seen her before in my life.' Connor then drank his coffee and swallowed hard because it was too hot and bitter. 'I've never seen anyone here before in my life except for you.' He drank again but it was still bitter. 'This needs sugar.'

'I'm just stressed,' she said.

'I know,' he said. He stirred his sugarless coffee with a spoon, letting it spin so that the bubbles looked like a galaxy. The spoon broke through the froth and sunk down to the bottom. 'It'll be over soon.'

'I just want to get it out the way. It's killing me.'

'Hey, did you know people with green eyes are supposed to be magical or something?'

'How?'

'I don't know,' he said. 'I read it somewhere. I think it's just a way of saying they're unique.'

'Isn't everyone unique?'

'Yeah, but it's just a nice thing, I think.' He pulled at the sleeves of his suit jacket. 'You know, people with green eyes normally stay together... you know... for a long time.'

'Oh really?'

'Yeah.'

'My friend Thomas stayed with his girlfriend for a few years,' she said. 'He has blue eyes.'

'Who's Thomas?'

'My friend.'

'I never heard of Thomas.'

'You wouldn't have. You don't know him.'

The noise of the café became louder as more people came in. A hundred smells at once; sweet, fragrant, sickly saccharine. There were a few people sitting outside with their coffees in the remaining sunlight.

'I know you're upset.'

Rachel looked at him. A slight stream of sunlight came in through the window and grazed her cheek until she moved her head down.

'I know you miss your brother.'

She didn't speak.

'This needs sugar,' he said. He got up from his seat and walked over to the counter. He picked up the glass sugar dispenser and began to pour some into his mug.

'Did you need sugar?' the waitress said.

'Yeah,' Connor said. 'I've got it, though.'

'I'm sorry,' she said.

'What for?'

58

'For not bringing the sugar over to you.'

'It's okay, I got it myself.'

'Your wife doesn't look too happy about it.'

'She's not my wife, she's my girlfriend,' he said. He looked over at Rachel. She glanced once then turned away. 'It's okay, though, she doesn't take sugar. Just me.'

'Oh. Well you're both dressed very smart.'

'Thank you.'

'You're dressed like you're going to a wedding.'

'Not a wedding.'

'Oh.'

'She wanted me to guess her eye colour,' he said. 'That's why her hands were over her eyes. She wasn't crying, she just wanted me to guess her eye colour.'

The waitress stared at him for a moment. 'Well,' she said, 'let me know if I can get you anything else.' She tried to smile but it wasn't enough. She instead seemed to glare. In doing so she just about opened up her soul to him; something he wasn't sure what he was seeing. Her eyes weren't green at all though, but a light shade of grey.

'Are you okay?' he said as she was about to walk away.

'Why would you ask me that?'

'I was just wondering.'

'Your girlfriend is waiting for you.'

'She thought you looked sad.'

The waitress sighed and placed her weight on one leg, making her hip jut like a catwalk model. She said, 'I'm sad because I work this fucking job. I'm sad because I have no money. I'm sad because I'm tired. I'm sad because the only man I ever loved went from my life three years ago. I'm sorry I can't hide it better. Would you like a food menu?'

'No thanks,' Connor said. As he went to walk away, the waitress spoke again.

'You both need each other, you know.' She then vanished as quickly as she'd appeared, through a door near the screeching metal arm of the espresso machine.

When he got back to the table, Rachel's coffee mug was empty. His was still full. He stirred it, now sweet with sugar.

'It'll be cold now,' Rachel said.

'It's fine.'

'Why were you talking to the waitress for so long?'

'She asked if we wanted food.'

'Oh. I thought you were complaining or something.'

'No,' he said. 'I was just getting the sugar.'

'You shouldn't have too much sugar,' she said. 'It'll make you fat.'

'I've been through this before,' he said. 'I know what it's like.'

'I know that.'

'It gets easier, you know?'

'I just hate wearing black.'

'I know.'

'Funerals make me feel like everything's coming to an end.'

'Not everything.'

'You don't know that.'

'I hate how noisy this place is.'

'Do you want to sit outside?'

'What?'

'I said, Do you want to sit outside?'

'Okay.'

They got up and Connor put some money onto the

table, taking his cold cappuccino with him. Rachel had walked ahead as Connor weaved through a crowd of people. He found them irritating. But as he passed each person, no one looked at him. He didn't want them to look at him, but it still felt lonely to not be noticed.

The quiet outside was gentle and solid like the slow sound of a violin. There were a few tables and chairs set up in the space in front of the café. Rachel wasn't there. Just a number of unrecognisable heads. Floating dismembered heads talking and drinking coffee. None of them seemed to be attached to bodies. Except for one. There was Rachel. She had a small table by the café window. She looked at him with an expression that he could only read as, 'Where've you been?' (However, it could also have meant, 'It was only ten seconds but I still missed you.')

He sat down with her. Drank his cold coffee.

'You don't like that,' she said.

'It's fine.'

'I can tell you don't like it.'

'Do you want another coffee?'

'No, thanks.'

'Beer? Wine?'

'No, thank you.'

'Are you sure?'

'Why do you do this to me, Connor? I'm sure you're trying to kill me. Do you want me dead or something?'

'What?'

'You drive me crazy and I think I'll end up dead.'

'You won't end up dead,' he said.

'Everyone dies,' she said. 'It scares me.' She looked at his coffee and began to bite her nails. 'Doesn't it scare you?'

'No. I'm not scared of dying,' he said. 'Never have

been.'

'Is there anything you *are* scared of?'

He paused. 'You,' he said.

She stopped biting her nails.

'I know I say the wrong thing sometimes, but I try.'

The sun caught her eyes and they were the greenest he'd ever seen. He smiled. Drank his cold coffee.

'What's wrong with you?' she said.

'I'm just an absolute idiot,' he said.

'I could have told you that.'

She stood up and motioned for him to stand up too. She fixed his black tie. Pulled it so he felt it tight around his neck. Then she loosened it slightly for him.

'You look nice,' he said.

She smiled.

'You *do*,' he said.

'I don't like wearing dresses.'

'Even black ones?'

'Even black ones.'

'So, do you think I should get a haircut or not?'

'If you want,' she said. 'I just worry you'll look completely different and you won't be you anymore.'

'I'll always be me. I think.'

'Okay.'

'You want to get a beer afterwards?'

'Yeah,' she said. 'I'd love one.'

On the table, the two coffee mugs were empty. Some people went in the café and some came out.

Her hands were still holding onto his tie as she looked at him and said, 'Your eyes are green too. Just like mine.'

Tell Me It Was Real. Tell Me It Happened

I went for a run down by the beach and saw the crows on the sand. Whenever they shrieked and called out it made me believe they were something else entirely. A completely different animal, like a whale. The sound took me right back to my childhood when I'd come up here and I'd had no idea where those sounds came from. It's hard to forget that sound.

One of the crows, a great black thing about the size of my head – I could almost smell it when it flew over me, a sweet smell like sugar – became its own silhouette against the white sky and the white sun. The only other colour was the tiny spark of its yellow beak.

I ran along the promenade. The tide was in, leaving only a small space for the sand. It was a cold morning. I was running to clear my head. Kate was at home, but she wouldn't be there when I got back. She was going to Scotland where she'd start a new job and a new life. I wasn't going with her. She'd been excited about this for weeks, and over those weeks as I'd thought about it, I knew I didn't want to go. It was her life, not mine.

When I run, I lose my thoughts like dropping things out of my pockets. My chest ached but it wasn't my heart, I just found it difficult to breathe, and soon that ache shot through my thighs and my calves. My feet were bits of rusting machinery coming undone.

The more I ran, the more I felt like I was doing something right, even though everything was wrong. Soon Kate would be gone. Five years gone. We'd met outside the pub in the middle of summer. I'd known her friend. That was the start of it. I still get images of her lying in bed, asleep, calm and displaced as though she were floating upstream. The water was green and grey; seaweed had collected at the edge like hair. Various flotsam – logs and small sticks – lay on the small patch of wet sand.

When I was near the far end of the promenade where the railing turned away from the beach and a wall of rocks lined the coast towards the lighthouse, I saw a girl in the water. The wind threw her voice to me but the waves were too rough to hear what she was saying.

I stopped running and tried to catch my breath. When I looked up again, I couldn't see her. I scanned the water, the green waves splashing white froth. The blank sky gave little light. I climbed over the railing and dropped down onto the sand to get a better look.

I saw her. She waved her arms pathetically for a few seconds before going back under. I realised she was about to drown, so I quickly took off my shoes and my hoodie and I ran into the sea until the sharp chill was up to my waist and I had to push hard against the current before I could begin to swim.

It was painfully cold and felt like a shock of electricity. I swam for what felt like much longer than it was. The more I swung my arms and kicked my legs, the further away she seemed. I felt the strength of the current as it pulled her further out. I didn't want it to pull us both, so I swam harder, gasping for breath, tasting the sharp salt of the sea. I caught glimpses of her between quick cold gasps, getting closer, her arms up, still waving, her voice louder and clearer.

When I was close enough, I grabbed hold of her. The tug from the fabric of her clothes heavy and awkward within my numb grip as she thrashed around, her arms flailing, slippery like a fish, though a warmness weakly beating through her cold skin.

'Help me! Please!' she yelled through mouthfuls of water. I hooked one arm around her chest and swam backwards with the other towards the shore. My muscles had tensed up, hardened to granite. Painful cramps at my shoulder and neck. She didn't say a word as I swam; she was either scared or in shock. Soon the water calmed as it thinned near the beach and I felt the sand beneath my feet.

She knelt on the sand, coughing, trying to catch her breath. I asked her how she was but she didn't answer. So I waited. As I waited, though, and I got a good look at her, I thought she looked just like my sister. I waited some more, not wanting to ask again, and when she was calm, she looked at me and said, 'Thank you.'

I thought of asking her *Are you my sister?* But I didn't. She wasn't my sister. I could see that. But it was uncanny how much she looked like her. The sharp line of jaw, hair the colour of brown sugar, blackened with water. But something else was odd about her, something which took my mind a second to register, I don't know why, it was as though the image of her rested in my mind like a dream and it was hard to see straight, my thoughts entangled and blurred. She was wearing a red dress.

'You're welcome,' I said. 'What were you doing out there? The water's dangerous in this weather.'

'I didn't know it was dangerous.'

'And it's cold.'

'I know it's cold,' she said.

'What were you doing in the water?'

'Swimming,' she said.

We both sat on the hard wet sand, freezing cold. She was shivering and her lips were blue. I gave her my hoodie and she wrapped it around herself.

'Do you normally go out in the water when it's like this?'
I said. 'You probably should have waited until it gets warm.'

'Not often, no.'

'You should just wait until it gets warm,' I said. The red
of her dress was black and looked very heavy as though it was
dragging her down. She looked incredibly out-of-place. But still, I
couldn't believe how much she looked like my sister. But then it
made me think that she must have looked like me.

A crow flew overhead. I smelled its sweet sugar smell as
it flew over us then over the water before turning around. It
landed next to several other crows on the sand a little further up.
I could hear them shrieking.

'Where have you been?' I said. But she just looked at me.
I said, 'I mean because of the dress.'

'I was at a friend's wedding,' she said.

'What happened?'

'My friend got married,' she said.

'No, I mean because you were in the water.'

'What do you think happened?' she said.

I didn't know. I couldn't think why she'd be in the sea in
a red bridesmaid's dress, almost drowning in the freezing cold
water. I couldn't think why she looked like my sister either. I
couldn't think of anything in that moment, my mind had frozen
solid. For a moment, I'd even forgotten why I was out there. I had
been running. Then I remembered Kate, packing her bags that
very second.

The girl held my hoodie tightly, the hooks of her fingers
were blue like her lips and I was worried she'd get pneumonia.

'It was last night,' she said. 'It didn't end well.'

'Why didn't it end well?' I said.

'Because I ended up in the sea, why do you think?' Between her shivers, she took quick, shallow breaths. She stared down at the sand, then she looked up at the crows flying overhead. 'Why are *you* here?'

'I was running,' I said.

'In this weather?'

'I had to get out,' I said. 'My girlfriend is leaving. 'She'll be gone by the time I get back.'

'That's a shame,' she said. 'What happened?'

'It just didn't work out.'

'Yes, but *why*?'

'I don't know why,' I said. 'These things just happen.'

'Nothing just *happens*,' she said.

'She's going to start a new life up in Scotland,' I said. 'I'm not.'

I stood up and helped her to her feet. Her hands were small lumps of ice. I thought it best if she got out of the cold. Our clothes were soaking. I began to feel the cold more than before; the adrenaline must have worn off. As we walked along the sand, the crows flew away.

'I'm sorry that happened to you,' she said. 'With you and your girlfriend.' I didn't thank her, but I looked at her to see if she would speak again. Her hair was black and slick as if made out of oil. Her hair was the same colour as the crows.

We let the cold air dry us. I felt my fingers freezing in my pockets. I was colder now without my hoodie, which was keeping her warm. The water, distant now, boiled in the winter air, frustrated it didn't get to take one of us. Kate was terrified of the sea. She was scared of drowning so she never learnt to swim. When I look out at the sea, I imagine it's a place where she is not.

'You look just like my sister,' I said.

'Do I?' she said.

'Yeah,' I said.

'What does your sister look like?'

'A bit like me, I think.'

'Oh right,' she said. 'Yeah, I suppose.' The shiver was going from her voice. 'Where's your sister now?'

'She moved away, not seen her in years.'

'Where did she go?'

'London, last time I heard.'

'Last time you heard?'

'She's a musician. It's hard to keep up, but she's got her own life. She's not a kid anymore.'

'Wouldn't it be strange if I told you I was a musician too,' the girl said.

'Are you a musician?'

'No,' she laughed. 'I just work in an office.'

'I've never seen anyone swimming here before,' I said. 'We don't really have the climate for it. It can get hot in the summer, though.' We climbed back up onto the promenade. 'I hope you don't do it again.'

'I won't,' she said. The wind blew cold and hard and the water rushed up the sand creating a huge dark patch where we'd just been sitting. 'You should call your sister. The musician. I bet she'd like that, if you called her.'

'Yeah probably,' I said. 'But it's been a while. Don't you have a sister? Or a brother?'

'I don't have any brothers or sisters,' she said. 'I always wondered what it would be like to have siblings. They always say, don't they, only child's are crazy.' She laughed.

The sand banks turned to bramble and weeds as we moved away along the promenade. The weeds smelled of vinegar

68

and urine. In the distance, the shrieking crows made dancing swoops beneath the low-hanging clouds. They were just crumbs of black pepper.

'I have a cousin,' she said. 'But I've not seen him in years either.'

'Why not?'

'There was something wrong with him,' she said. 'He had issues. Well, that's what they called it. "Issues." Sounds like something that was given to him. I don't know, just this label he had that he couldn't get rid of. I felt bad for him. We were friends for a couple of years when we were younger. We used to go to the park with the other kids in the neighbourhood. He knew this girl who always smoked, you could smell it on her, a hot sour smell. She smoked from when she was twelve years old; her mum used to buy cigarettes for her. She and my cousin started dating when they were teenagers. Apparently, he tried to force himself on her, but no one really believed her because of the smell, like she couldn't be trusted, and neither could her mother. We stopped hanging out together after that.

'One day, he walked into a church. I don't know why; my family isn't religious or anything. He just sat there, facing the altar, until he broke down crying. A friend of my dad saw him there, asked him if he was okay, but my cousin took one look at him and left. Never really heard from him after that.'

'Did he have a religious experience or something?'

'Maybe. He had issues. My guess is that he's in prison somewhere now.'

We reached the path that turned off from the promenade, which eventually led to the road. The sand under our feet became sparse and dusty. Further ahead, I could see the shapes of buildings, and one was the spire of a disused church. I knew

69

people did that, broke down crying for no reason at all. I'd caught Kate doing that once. She'd been listening to a song, standing in the middle of the living room crying. She became irritated that I'd seen her crying. Can't for the life of me remember what the song was, though.

'It's probably the last time I'll see my girlfriend, Kate,' I said.

'Yeah,' the girl said. 'Sometimes you don't even know your own family, as much as you love them. That's not to say they're bad people. Life and love are two separate things.'

When we reached the road, the girl said she was going home and said she was fine now, that she didn't need any more help. I let her keep the hoodie.

When I got home, Kate was gone. All her things were gone too. I physically felt the emptiness there like a swelling mass in my chest. That evening, I called my sister. She was happy to hear from me. We talked for some time, laughing about the things we got up to when we were younger, and she told me about her music career and the band. She then said this: 'Do you remember when we were kids and Mum and Dad used to take us down to the beach in the summer? And it was really hot, sweltering, it was so hot that I can remember how hot it was. I can still feel it. We walked along the promenade and the four of us stood at the railings before the sand and we looked out at the water, and everyone else was looking out at the water too. We looked out at the water and we saw dozens of whales there. Humpback whales. So many of them together. They were just there, in the sea, blowing water from their blowholes, and we all looked at them. I thought they were beautiful, and the sounds they made, like birds. But the thing is, I don't know if it was a dream or a memory. We don't get whales up there, do we? Tell me it was real. Tell me it happened.'

I lied and said, 'Yeah, there are whales there,' and she laughed down the phone from somewhere else in the country.

Acknowledgements

My thanks go to James Rice and Matthew Scully for the many writing workshops and beers over the years. To Lulu Taylor for the support and for reading what I wrote. To my friends and family. To everyone who read my writing. To those who taught me creative writing at UCLan and LJMU. And to all those I sat and had conversations with which inevitably inspired my stories.

Lightning Source UK Ltd.
Milton Keynes UK
UKHW011500060223
416538UK00004B/355